SWEET DREAMS,
LITTLE MONSTER

BY CAROLINE BENNETT

ISBN: 1978237987
ISBN-13: 978-1978237988

Sweet Dreams, Little Monster is the delightful tale of a friendly little monster being put to bed.

From learning that a bubble bath can be fun to brushing the beetles from his teeth, the young monster learns everything.

He uses a bug-flavored toothpaste and drinks hot slime for his bedtime drink, he even prays before bed, and then enjoys a bedtime story or two.

- *Written in an easy-to-read rhyming format*
- *Beautifully illustrated throughout*
- *Teaches children aged 4-8 about a bedtime routine*
- *Creatively written with a young audience in mind*

Children and adults alike will enjoy the captivating story of Sweet Dreams, Little Monster.

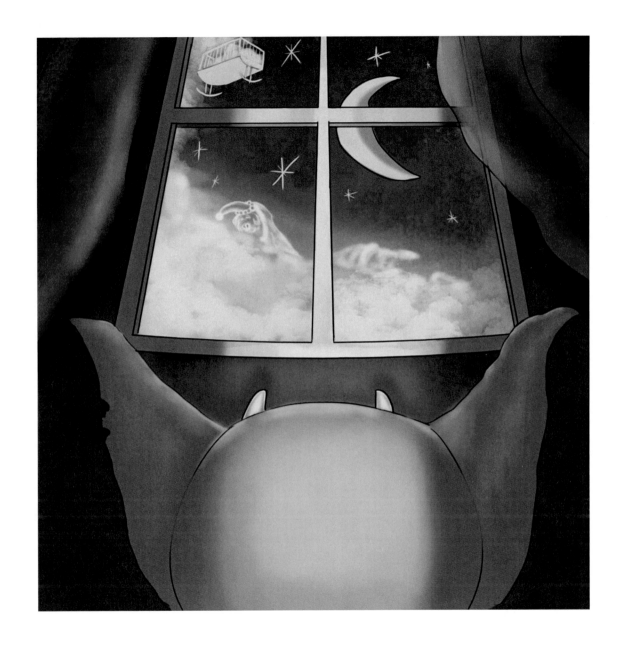

Little Monster, the nighttime is here,
It's growing dark, there's nothing to fear,

Time for bed, so we must prepare,

Come on, hop out of your armchair.

Into the bath, you must climb,

To wash away all the grime,

Raise your tail high up in the air,

So Mommy can scrub under there.

Your big ears need a clean and a scrub,

Stop fidgeting, you'll fall out of the tub,

Blow the bubbles, Little Monster, and laugh,

There's a lot of fun to have in the bath.

Here's your toy duck, bobbing around,

The one you always do knock down,

It's a lovely duck with a red beak,

Press his sides gently and hear him squeak.

Wrapped in a big towel, all soft and fluffy,

Even after a bath, you still look scruffy!

Little Monster, all you do is fidget,

I need to dry your toes—every digit.

Let's get you dressed in pajamas all clean,

Your favorite yellow pair with stripes of green,

Little Monster, I'll get your scales all dry,

Come and sit on my lap, my little guy.

I'll fix you a cup of hot slime to sip,

But be careful now, not to burn your lip,

You burnt it last time and then you cried,

It took hours for your tears to be dried.

So blow and blow on it until it's cool,

Make sure it is and don't act like a fool,

Just sip at the slime slowly and enjoy,

Its banana flavored, my monster boy.

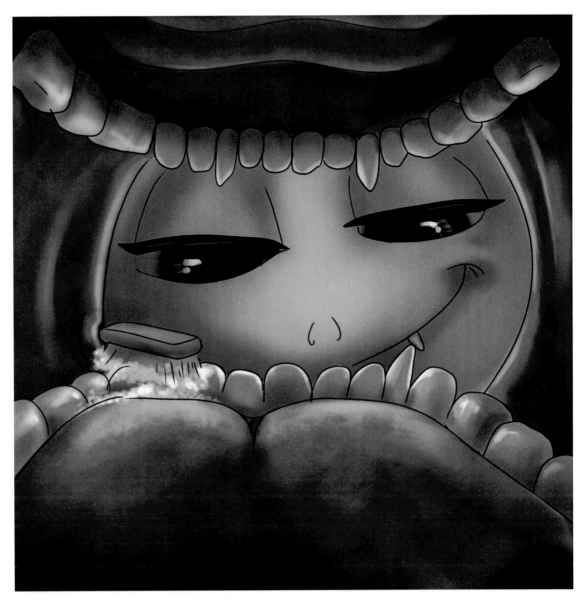

Now we have all your teeth to brush,

No need to hurry or to rush,

Open up wide so Mommy can see,

Exactly where the toothbrush should be.

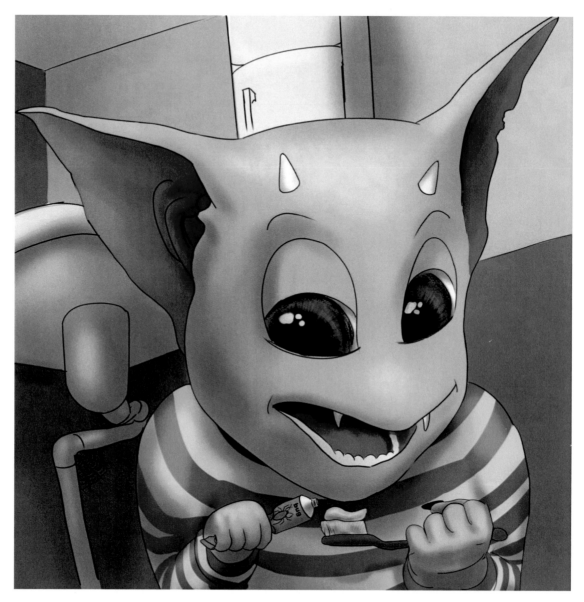

A bug-flavored toothpaste is what we use,

It's so tasty and good, it's on the news,

Make sure you brush them properly and well,

You were eating worms with their yucky smell.

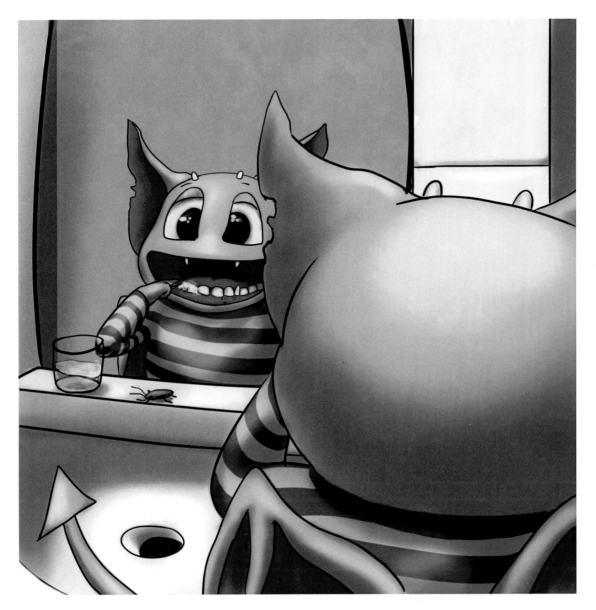

I heard you crunching beetles, too,

The ones with six legs that are blue,

Make sure you brush at the back,

Or else your teeth will turn black.

Ready for bed now at long last,

It takes time and is never fast,

There's a lot to do before bed,

Before your story can be read.

You know what to do before sleep,

Close your eyes and pray, but don't peep,

Give thanks for the day and being well,

And then a bedroom story I'll tell.

Here's your story, snuggle under your quilt,

The tale of three pigs and their houses built,

One straw, one bricks, and one from sticks,

And a mean bad wolf up to his tricks.

The strongest house is made from brick,

It's the last one the wolf does pick,

All the pigs are okay and survive,

To live their lives happy and alive.

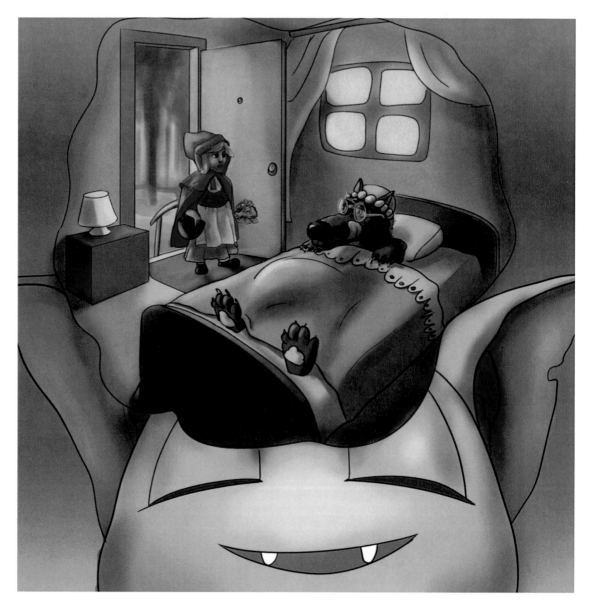

Then there's the tale of Red Riding Hood,

Who goes to see Grandma in the wood,

The Big Bad Wolf does trick her to believe,

That he is her grandma, he does deceive.

Don't worry, Little Monster, don't fret,

The story ends happy, so don't sweat,

Most stories have a happy ever after,

Then the children's bedrooms are full of laughter.

They fall asleep as happy as can be,

And sleep through until the morning you see,

You'll do this, Little Monster of mine,

You'll have sweet dreams that are just so fine.

So I'll tuck you in and wish you goodnight,

As you sleep with the stars and the moonlight,

Goodnight, Little Monster, do have sweet dreams,

Where all is truly as good as it seems

Thank you for purchasing this book!

If you and your child liked this book, please, <u>leave a positive feedback on Amazon</u>. It is extremely important for us.

Made in the USA
San Bernardino, CA
18 March 2018